To Jennifer

STORY
KELLEY ARMSTRONG

ART
XAVIERE DAUMARIE

COLORS
LOWENAEL + XAVIERE DAUMARIE

For all the readers who wanted more Reese,
this one's for you.

-K.A.

Huge thanks to:
Kelley Armstrong for being so wonderful and adventurous enough
to agree to this crazy project,
Bill, Yanni and Gail from SubterraneanPress for saying yes to the first limited edition
and being so supportive,
Rachel Zimra and Lowenael, my partners in comics,
Megan Kearney, Meaghan Carter and the ladies of the Comic Book Embassy of Toronto,
for being the amazing and inspiring artists they are.
My family and loved ones, always.

Xavière

Story and Characters
Copyright (c) 2015 by KLA Fricke, Inc

Illustrations
Copyright (c) 2015 by Xaviere Daumarie

Second edition published in 2016
First limited edition published in 2015 by SubterraeanPress

All rights reserved.

GOODBYE, MISS MADDIE. ALWAYS A PLEASURE.

ONE OF THESE DAYS...

THEY WANTED--

SOMETHING. I KNOW. THEY ALWAYS WANT SOMETHING.

IT'S THE PRICE WE PAY FOR LIVING IN AUSTRALIA, MADDIE. I CAN'T STAY ON THEIR TURF WITHOUT PAYING MY DUES. IT'S THAT OR JOIN THE PACK. AND IF I JOIN THE PACK...

I HAVE THE BLOOD. THAT MAKES ME VALUABLE BREEDING STOCK.

IT'S GOTTEN A LOT WORSE SINCE I GREW UP. MAYBE IF I MOVED OUT--

ABSOLUTELY NOT. THEY'D GRAB YOU AS SOON AS THEY THOUGHT I WASN'T WATCHING. WE'LL WORK THIS OUT. WE ALWAYS DO.

IT SOUNDS LIKE A BOUNTY CASE.

IT IS, WHICH IS WHY THEY BROUGHT IT TO ME. GOT THE BEST NOSE IN THE BUSINESS.

IN THIS CASE, THE LAWS THE KID BROKE WERE PACK LAWS. SOUNDS LIKE A REAL PIECE OF WORK, TOO. WENT AFTER THE OLD ALPHA'S DAUGHTER, WHO'S NOW THE NEW ALPHA'S MATE. I DON'T LIKE DOING THE PACK'S DIRTY WORK, BUT THIS IS ONE WOLF I DON'T MIND TURNING OVER TO THEM.

WELL, AT LEAST I GOT THE DOSE RIGHT THIS TIME.

SWEET DREAMS, DAD.

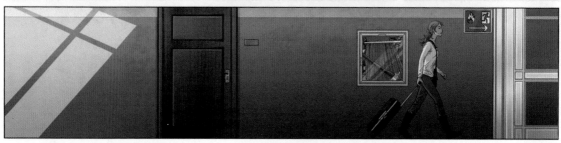

NEW YORK, NEWARK AIRPORT

I'M SURE YOU'VE HAD FUN IN THE BIG APPLE, REESE...

BUT IT'S TIME TO COME HOME.

ELENA, HEY. WHAT'S UP?

THANK YOU, ELENA.

LEFT YOUR CELL IN YOUR ROOM AGAIN?

REESE, YOU HAVE CLASSES THIS WEEK, RIGHT?

UNFORTUNATELY.

GOOD. I GOT A MESSAGE THROUGH THE SUPERNATURAL GRAPEVINE ABOUT A POSSIBLE WEREWOLF SIGHTING ON CAMPUS AT COLUMBIA.

UH, THAT'S NOT ME, GUARANTEED. I DON'T DO ANYTHING THAT WOULD EVEN HINT--

I KNOW. I'M JUST ASKING YOU TO CHECK IT OUT. I CAN'T IMAGINE A MUTT TRESPASSING ON PACK TERRITORY THAT BLATANTLY, BUT IT'S WORTH A QUICK CHECK, IF YOU'RE THERE ALREADY.

I'LL GET ON IT.

IF THERE'S A WEREWOLF HERE, I'D BETTER FIND HIM. FAST. BEFORE HE MAKES A MISTAKE HE'LL NEVER STOP REGRETTING.

I WAS AN IDIOT.

ANOTHER WEREWOLF ON CAMPUS? THE CHANCES SEEM NEXT TO NIL, ESPECIALLY ON THE PACK'S HOME TURF. BUT I DIDN'T EXPECT TROUBLE WHEN I WENT TO UNI BACK HOME, EVEN IF THE AUSTRALIAN PACK HAD A BOUNTY ON MY FATHER. IT'S UNI. HOW WOULD THEY FIND ME THERE?

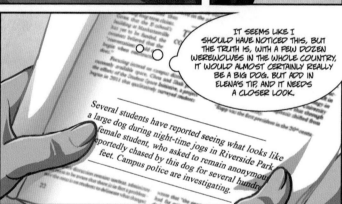

IT SEEMS LIKE I SHOULD HAVE NOTICED THIS, BUT THE TRUTH IS, WITH A FEW DOZEN WEREWOLVES IN THE WHOLE COUNTRY, IT WOULD ALMOST CERTAINLY REALLY BE A BIG DOG. BUT ADD IN ELENA'S TIP, AND IT NEEDS A CLOSER LOOK.

Several students have reported seeing what looks like a large dog during night-time jogs in Riverside Park. [female] student, who asked to remain anonymous, reportedly chased by this dog for several hundred feet. Campus police are investigating.

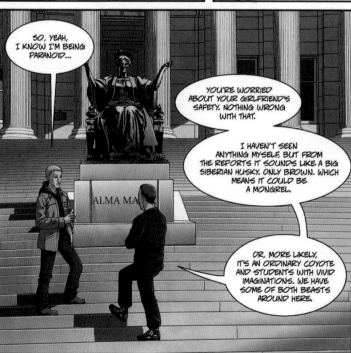

SO, YEAH, I KNOW I'M BEING PARANOID...

YOU'RE WORRIED ABOUT YOUR GIRLFRIEND'S SAFETY. NOTHING WRONG WITH THAT.

I HAVEN'T SEEN ANYTHING MYSELF, BUT FROM THE REPORTS IT SOUNDS LIKE A BIG SIBERIAN HUSKY. ONLY BROWN. WHICH MEANS IT COULD BE A MONGREL.

OR, MORE LIKELY, IT'S AN ORDINARY COYOTE AND STUDENTS WITH VIVID IMAGINATIONS. WE HAVE SOME OF BOTH BEASTS AROUND HERE.

ALMA MA[TER]

I BET. BUT IF I WANT TO SUGGEST MY GIRLFRIEND AVOIDS A CERTAIN AREA ON HER NIGHTLY RUNS, IS THERE ONE SPOT IN PARTICULAR...

SEEMS TO BE. ALL THE SIGHTINGS WERE JUST OFF CAMPUS, OVER BY...

MORNINGSIDE PARK

IT TOOK OFF. YOU'RE RIGHT-- IT WAS HUGE. A WOLFHOUND OR SOMETHING.

ARE YOU OKAY?

JUST... SHAKEN UP.

YEAH, I CAN IMAGINE.

IT DIDN'T BITE YOU, DID IT?

NO, THAT WAS A KILLER TREE BRANCH ATTACK.

LET'S GET YOU HOME.

THANKS FOR DOING THIS. I KNOW IT'S NOT A FUN WAY TO SPEND YOUR EVENINGS.

WHICH YOU ARE NEVER GOING TO DO AGAIN, RIGHT?

BETTER THAN HAVING YOU OUT HERE ALONE, AS A HUMAN, GOING AFTER MUTTS IN WOLF FORM.

YEAH.

WAS SHE CUTE?

DIDN'T NOTICE.

Sigh.

THAT'S THE FIERCEST CANINE WE'VE SEEN IN THREE NIGHTS. I THINK WE CAN SAFELY SAY THE MUTT IS LONG GONE.

JUST SOME KID. TOO YOUNG AND DUMB TO KNOW BETTER.

I WISH I BELIEVED THAT. BUT IT'S A LITTLE TOO COINCIDENTAL, A MUTT SHOWING UP AT MY SCHOOL.

ELENA KNOWS MY PAST. SHE A LITTLE CONCERNED, BUT NOT ENOUGH TO RACE DOWN HERE WITH CLAY. WHICH MEANS SHE'S PRETTY SURE IT'S NOT RELATED TO ME.

I HOPE SO. THINGS ARE FINALLY GOING RIGHT. I'D LIKE TO KEEP IT THAT WAY.

YOU'D BETTER NOT BE CUTTING CLASS, WILLIAMS. IT WASN'T EASY GETTING YOUR SCHEDULE.

ESPECIALLY WHEN YOU GO BY, REESE ANDERSON THESE DAYS.

HEY, THERE! I'VE BEEN LOOKING FOR YOU.

WELL, THIS IS A PROBLEM, ISN'T IT, BRAT?

WOULD YOU LIKE TO SEE YOUR MOMMY AGAIN? LET ME SEND YOU--

FUCK!

YOU LITTLE BITCH!

MY FATHER WAS THERE FOR ME WHEN I NEEDED HIM. WILL I BE THERE FOR HIM NOW?

ABSOLUTELY.

REESE?

I--I NEED HELP.

W-WHAT?

YOU'RE SICK. I WAS TAKING YOU TO EMERGENCY. IF YOU WANT ME TO CALL SOMEONE--

NO, PLEASE. I NEED HELP. SOMETHING'S WRONG. Y--YOU ASKED IF THAT DOG BIT ME. I LIED.

WHAT?

IT--IT BIT ME. THE DOG. I DIDN'T WANT RABIES SHOTS. I KNOW THAT'S STUPID. NOW I'M SO SICK.

PLEASE. HELP ME.

YOU KNOW, I MIGHT HAVE BOUGHT IT IF YOU WERE A LITTLE SMARTER. OR IF YOU EXPECTED ME TO BE SMARTER.

WH-WHAT?

I'M SO SICK.

THEN YOU SHOULD HAVE INSISTED I TAKE YOU TO A HOSPITAL.

WHAT?

YOU'RE SICK AND YOU LET SOME GUY YOU BARELY KNOW TAKE YOU TO A MOTEL.

MAYBE I'M NOT THINKING STRAIGHT. I'VE GOT A FEVER AND--

WHO THE HELL ARE YOU?

I DON'T WANT TO HURT YOU, BUT YOU ARE GOING TO TALK TO ME. STOP--

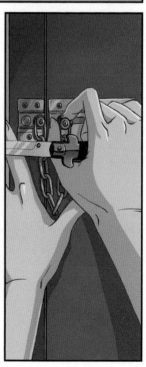

DAMN IT,
EVEN AFTER DANIELLA,
ALL IT TAKES IS A FEW TEARS,
AND I FEEL LIKE A MONSTER
AND BACK OFF.

FINE! JUST STAY THERE AND TALK TO ME. I WON'T COME ANY CLOSER.

GODDAMN IT!

NFFFF

I KNOW BY YOUR SCENT WHAT YOU ARE. WHAT YOUR FATHER IS.

HELLO?

REESE?
WHAT'S WRONG?

REESE?
TROUBLE?

HE'S AT HOME.
IT'S FINE. GO BACK
TO SLEEP.

OKAY.
TELL ME WHAT
HAPPENED.

YOU'RE CERTAIN SHE'S A WEREWOLF'S DAUGHTER?

NO, I'M SURE THE SCENT IS WEAK. THERE'S NO WAY YOU COULD HAVE KNOWN EARLIER. DON'T BEAT YOURSELF UP OVER THIS.

YOU'RE GOING TO HAVE TO TELL EVERYONE WHAT HAPPENED IN AUSTRALIA.

MOMMY? WAS THAT REESE? IS HE OKAY?

HE'S FINE. HE JUST NEEDS TO DO SOMETHING VERY HARD.

AND MOM AND DAD NEED TO GO HELP HIM.

I'M STARTING TO THINK YOU DON'T WANT TO CATCH THIS MONGREL, MADDIE. IS THAT IT? YOU THINK HE'S CUTE?

NO, I THINK HE'S SMARTER THAN KEITH AND DANIELLA FIGURED. WARIER, AT LEAST.

REESE KNOWS HE'S ON YOUR PACK'S HIT LIST. EVEN ON THE OTHER SIDE OF THE WORLD, HE HASN'T LOWERED HIS GUARD.

THEN YOU NEED TO LOWER IT FOR HIM.

YOU'RE HURTING HER, RAY. THAT WON'T HELP. LET HER GO.

FROM NOW ON? WE WORK TOGETHER.

OTHERWISE I TELL KEITH YOU'VE RUN. HE'LL TAKE IT OUT ON YOUR DADDY.

DON'T WORRY. I HAVE AN IDEA. WE'LL TALK AT THE MOTEL.

JASON, IT'S CHARLIE. I HEARD WHAT HAPPENED TONIGHT. I NEED YOU TO TALK TO KEITH.

OBVIOUSLY MADDIE CAN'T DO THIS. SHE'S JUST A KID. YOU'RE GOING TO NEED TO GRAB THE GUY YOURSELF.

I KNOW I STILL OWE THE MONEY. TELL KEITH I'LL PAY IT BACK. WITH INTEREST. I'M SORRY. I REALLY THOUGHT THIS WOULD WORK.

DAD SET ME UP. THIS WASN'T ABOUT SAVING ME FROM THE PACK. IT WAS ABOUT SAVING HIMSELF FROM A DEBT.

I'LL SEE YOU GUYS IN CLASS.

WHO'S THE CHICK?

NO IDEA

GIVE HER MY NUMBER?

I WASN'T TRYING TO GET AWAY.

HUH, SURE LOOKED LIKE IT.

I JUST WANT TO TALK TO YOU-- WITHOUT BEING PINNED TO A WALL.

YOU COME AFTER REESE? THIS IS THE ONLY WAY WE'RE TALKING.

DRRRRRRIIIIING

I KNOW YOU HAVE TO GO, BUT I REALLY DO WANT TO TALK.

HOW ABOUT LATER? SOMEPLACE MORE PRIVATE?

TAKE THIS AND MEET ME THERE.

JUST TELL ME WHEN AND WHERE.

NO, TAKE THIS. TO BE SURE.

SORRY I'M LATE.

WHAT DID YOU WANT TO TALK ABOUT?

IS THIS FAR ENOUGH? NO ONE'S OUT HERE. I CAN TELL, YOU KNOW. I--

UM, LET'S GO A LITTLE FURTHER.

WHATEVER.

ASKING TO
MEET ME IN
PRIVATE?

YOU REALLY DO
THINK I'M STUPID IF YOU
EXPECTED ME TO
COME ALONE.

AND YOU MUST
THINK I'M STUPID IF YOU
EXPECTED ME TO
COME ALONE.

I DON'T BLAME YOU FOR TRYING BUT...

YOU'RE SURROUNDED BY FIVE WEREWOLVES.

IF I WERE YOU, I'D SAVE MY ENERGY.

YOU'RE GOING TO NEED IT FOR THE NEXT PART.

I DON'T KNOW HOW MUCH GOSSIP YOU HEAR IN AUSTRALIA.

BUT WHEN IT COMES TO INTERROGATIONS, CLAY'S AN EXPERT.

NOT MUCH FOR ENTERTAINMENT, I'M AFRAID.

I DON'T SPEND MUCH TIME IN HERE.

WEREWOLVES ARE SOCIAL BEASTS. I KNOW.

YEAH, I GUESS YOU DO.

ANYWAY, THE MAIN THING IS THAT YOU'RE SAFE HERE.

I'D FEEL BETTER ABOUT THAT IF MY PLAN WORKED, AND YOU HAD JASON AND RAY IN CUSTODY.

IF THEY STAYED AWAY BECAUSE THEY SMELLED A SETUP...

YOU LET US WORRY ABOUT THAT.

WE'RE DISCUSSING IT RIGHT NOW.

I COULD HELP WITH THAT.

ELENA SAID NO. JUST BECAUSE YOU DIDN'T ACTUALLY KIDNAP NOAH DOESN'T MEAN THEY TRUST YOU.

ESPECIALLY WHEN YOU DID PLAN TO KIDNAP ME.

I--

WE'LL TALK LATER.

...OBVIOUSLY I NEED TO TALK ABOUT WHAT HAPPENED IN AUSTRALIA.

AS DIFFICULT AS IT IS.

IF YOU DON'T WANT TO, IT CAN WAIT. WE ALL TRUST YOU.

IT'S NOT AN ISSUE OF TRUST. EVERYONE NEEDS TO KNOW EXACTLY WHAT'S GOING ON.

ELENA'S RIGHT. SO THE PROBLEM STARTED BEFORE I WAS BORN...

WHEN MY MOM WAS IN COLLEGE, SHE WAS ATTACKED BY THREE MUTTS. SHE ESCAPED, RAN TO THE AUTHORITIES AND TOLD HER STORY.

NO ONE BELIEVED HER, OF COURSE. BUT THE AUSTRALIAN PACK COULDN'T TAKE THAT CHANCE. THEY SENT MY DAD TO KILL HER.

INSTEAD OF KILLING HER, HE RAN OFF WITH HER, PUTTING THEM ON THE PACK'S MOST WANTED LIST.

FAST FORWARD TWENTY YEARS. I'M AT UNI. I CATCH TWO GUYS ATTACKING A GIRL IN AN ALLEY. OF COURSE I INTERFERE.

I FALL FOR THE GIRL. SHE FALLS FOR ME.

HELLO, REESE. THANK YOU FOR THE WEDDING GIFT.

THEY GOT DAD IN THE BARN. HE MADE IT TO THE HOUSE, AND WHEN MY MOTHER REALIZED WHAT WAS HAPPENING, SHE SENT ME A TEXT TO STAY AWAY. THEN SHE KILLED HERSELF.

DANIELLA SET ME UP TO WIN KEITH FOR HERSELF. I LED THEM TO MY PARENTS. THEY DIED BECAUSE I WAS STUPID AND CARELESS. AND I RAN, BECAUSE IT WAS ALL I COULD DO.

I WANT REVENGE, AND OBVIOUSLY THEY KNOW IT, SO THEY TRACKED ME HERE--

BZZZ-BZZZ-BZZZ

BIP

YOU HUNG UP ON HIM? THEY'VE KIDNAPPED MY--

SHE'LL HANDLE IT.

BZZZ BZZZZ

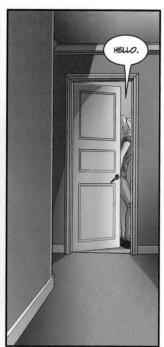

HELLO.

SO THEY HAVE YOUR DAD.

YES.

EITHER THEY BROUGHT HIM OVER OR...

OR HE CAME WITH THEM AND THIS IS A SETUP.

HONESTLY?

I DON'T KNOW WHAT TO THINK.

IT'S WHAT WE'D EXPECT.

WE GIVE THEM REESE; THEY GIVE US MADISON'S DAD.

REALLY? AND WE'RE SUPPOSED TO GIVE A FUCK ABOUT SOME AUSTRALIAN MUTT?

SORRY.

NO, HE'S RIGHT.

THEY ALSO PROMISE THAT IF WE HAND OVER REESE, THEY'LL GO AWAY AND NOT HURT US.

OH, WELL, IN THAT CASE...

ARE THEY SERIOUS?

YES, BUT ONLY BECAUSE THEY SEEM TO UNDERESTIMATE HOW MUCH WE'LL FIGHT FOR REESE.

THEY THINK YOU'LL HAND HIM OVER BECAUSE THEY WOULD, IF HE WAS THEIR NEW RECRUIT.

WHICH IS THE DIFFERENCE BETWEEN US.

ONE OF MANY.

BUT THE DEAL REMAINS AND IT'S APPARENTLY NON-NEGOTIABLE.

SO THE ANSWER'S OBVIOUS. WE TAKE REESE. PRETEND TO HAND HIM OVER. KICK ASS.

NO.

HUH?

THAT IS THE OBVIOUS ANSWER, WHICH MEANS IT'LL BE EXACTLY WHAT THEY EXPECT.

HERE'S THE PLAN...

NICE PLACE.

NICE ASS.

THAT THE BEST YOU CAN DO?

YOU SURE THESE GUYS ARE SMART ENOUGH TO HANDLE THIS, DARLING?

UM, MISSING SOMEONE, AREN'T YOU?

LOOKS LIKE YOU ARE, TOO.

I'VE DECIDED TO DECLINE YOUR OFFER.

AND WHAT DOES THE REAL ALPHA SAY?

SHE'D SAY YOU'RE AN IDIOT, BUT SHE'S TOO POLITE.

YOU THINK EVERYONE HASN'T FIGURED OUT THIS GAME THE AMERICAN PACK IS PLAYING?

MAKE CLAYTON DANVERS THE ALPHA AND YOU'D HAVE PANIC AND REVOLT.

PRETEND IT'S HIS MATE AND THEY ALL RELAX.

AND IT COULDN'T POSSIBLY BE HER?

A WOMAN? AS ALPHA?

I'D CALL THEM NEANDERTHALS, IF IT WASN'T AN INSULT TO NEANDERTHALS.

HUMOR US THEN.

THE POINT IS THAT YOU AREN'T GETTING REESE.

IF THAT'S A PROBLEM...

THEN THAT'S A PROBLEM.

I'M NOT SURE WHAT I HATE THE MOST.

BEING LEFT ON THE SIDELINES.

BEING LEFT HERE BY ANOTHER WOMAN.

OR KNOWING SHE'S RIGHT.

IF I'M IN THERE FIGHTING, THEY WON'T TREAT ME AS ANOTHER WOLF.

THEY'LL TREAT ME AS A HOSTAGE OR A PRIZE.

ELENA KNOWS THAT.

SO I'M OUT HERE, WITH ORDERS TO DRIVE OFF AT THE FIRST SIGN OF TROUBLE.

AND I HATE IT.

I'M SURE SHE KNOWS THAT TOO.

I JUST--

BAM

DAD?

WIIIZ

MADDIE? LET ME IN. WE HAVE TO GO. THE AMERICANS HELPED--

I KNOW WHAT YOU DID.

I GOT THE MESSAGE YOU LEFT FOR JASON.

ABOUT THE MONEY.

THAT'S WHAT THIS JOB WAS. PAYBACK FOR MONEY YOU OWED THEM.

IT WAS, BUT... NOT LIKE THAT. I DIDN'T BORROW FROM THEM, MADDIE. I'M NOT STUPID.

JUST LET ME IN. I'LL EXPLAIN ON THE WAY.

YOU'LL EXPLAIN NOW.

SIX MONTHS AGO THEY TOLD ME KEITH NEEDED MONEY.

IF I PAID THEM TWENTY GRAND, THEY'D LEAVE YOU ALONE FOR GOOD.

IT WAS A TRAP. I HAD THE MONEY, IT DISAPPEARED, AND THEY DEMANDED THE BOY INSTEAD.

SO THIS WAS ALL ABOUT GETTING REESE?

NO, IT SEEMS THAT WAS ONLY HALF THE PLAN. THEY'D GET HIM AND KEEP ME. YOU WANTED TO SAVE MY LIFE?

YOU'D MATE JASON.

I MATE HIM. ONLY THE ALPHA CAN MATE IN THEIR PACK.

BUT YOU'RE STILL SUITABLE FOR PROCREATION.

WHAT YEAR IS THIS? 1809?

IN THEIR WORLD, IT'S ALWAYS 1809, AT LEAST WHEN IT COMES TO WOMEN.

YOU'RE PRETTY, SMART, STRONG AND YOU HAVE WEREWOLF BLOOD. THEY'LL NEVER STOP PURSUING YOU.

I SHOULD HAVE SEEN THAT.

ALL I WANT IS FOR YOU TO BE SAFE, MADDIE.

IF THAT MEANS YOU DRIVE OFF NOW, ALONE, THEN DO THAT. PLEASE. JUST GO.

WHAT ARE YOU--?

I'M GOING TO HELP THEM.

THIS HAS NOTHING TO DO WITH US.

NO, IT HAS EVERYTHING TO DO WITH ME, DAD.

AND EVEN IF IT DIDN'T?

I WANT TO HELP.

I KNOW THAT'S NOT YOUR WAY. YOU DON'T GET INVOLVED.

BUT I NEED TO GET INVOLVED.

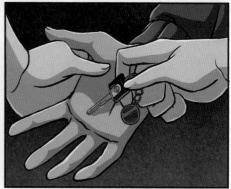

CAN YOU EVEN SEE THE DAMNED CABIN FROM HERE?

YES, BUT THE IMPORTANT THING IS THAT WE'RE CLOSE ENOUGH TO HEAR OUR CUE.

I WOULDN'T COUNT ON IT. OR ON BEING ABLE TO GET THERE IN TIME.

WE SHOULD BE CLOSER.

YOU'RE NOT EVEN GOING TO RESPOND TO THAT, ARE YOU?

NOPE. YOU KNOW WHY WE'RE WAY OUT HERE. BECAUSE YOU'RE THE TARGET.

THEY FIND YOU? MIGHT AS WELL GRAB YOU AND RUN.

WE SHOULD HAVE GONE WHEN WE HEARD THAT COMMOTION.

ANTONIO HANDLED IT, WHATEVER IT WAS. AS LONG AS THAT CABIN'S QUIET, WE STAY--

WHISTLE

AND THAT'S OUR SIGN. GUESS THEY DECIDED NOT TO NEGOTIATE.

BAM

AND THAT'S WHERE I HAVE TO STOP YOU, REESE.

HIS BROTHER KILLED MY PARENTS. HE WAS THERE. HE HELPED.

AND AS MUCH AS I HATE TO SAY THIS...

THAT HAS NOTHING TO DO WITH OUR PACK.

WHICH MEANS WE CAN'T RETALIATE FOR IT WITHOUT STARTING A WAR.

THEN LEAVE HIM WITH ME. GO OUT AND HELP THE OTHERS.

IS THAT AN ORDER?

NO, SORRY. I--

I KNOW WHAT YOU WANT. I CAN'T GIVE IT TO YOU. AND I'M SORRY FOR THAT.

...SO THAT WAS THEIR GRAND PLAN.

YOU WERE GOING TO FORCE MADISON TO HAVE YOUR BABIES?

HOW THE HELL DID YOU THINK THAT WOULD WORK OUT?

SHE'D HAVE GOTTEN USED TO THE IDEA.

NO, PRETTY SURE SHE WOULDN'T HAVE. IDIOT.

THE REASON YOU'RE LEAVING HERE ALIVE IS BECAUSE I DON'T WANT A WAR.

AND THE ONLY REASON I DON'T WANT A WAR IS BECAUSE I DON'T WANT THE HASSLE OF LEADING A SECOND PACK HALFWAY AROUND THE WORLD.

YOU'LL TELL KEITH THAT.

AND YOU'LL TELL HIM IF I EVER CATCH ONE OF HIS WOLVES TRESPASSING...

I'LL TAKE THAT AS A DECLARATION OF WAR, AND I GUESS I'LL START FIGURING OUT HOW TO ALPHA LONG-DISTANCE.

REESE IS OURS. YOU'LL FORGET HIM. WE'LL FORGET YOU.

CLAY? I THINK THEY NEED A GOING AWAY PRESENT.

A BROKEN ARM IS ALWAYS A NICE PARTING GIFT.

DO THAT THEN. RIGHT FOREARMS.

YOU'LL STAY HERE IN ANTONIO'S GUEST HOUSE UNTIL WE'RE SURE JASON AND HIS CREW ARE GONE.

AFTER THAT, WE CAN PUT YOU UP FOR A WEEK OR SO. THEN YOU HAVE A CHOICE.

APPLY FOR MEMBERSHIP IN THE PACK OR FIND A PLACE TO LIVE OUTSIDE NEW YORK STATE.

I'VE SPENT MY LIFE AVOIDING GETTING RECRUITED.

BUT...

IT'S NOT REALLY ABOUT WHAT'S BEST FOR ME.

WE'LL TALK.

I'LL CALL JEREMY AND GET HIM DIGGING UP CHARLIE'S DOSSIER.

I WANT AS MUCH BACKGROUND AS I CAN GET BEFORE I MAKE ANY KIND OF OFFER.

IN THE MEANTIME...

I'LL TAKE NICK AND THE BOYS AND WE'LL MAKE SURE OUR FRIENDS HAVE HEADED BACK DOWN UNDER.

GOOD.

I'M HOPING DAD DECIDES TO STAY. IT WOULD BE GOOD FOR HIM.

ANYTHING WE SHOULD KNOW ABOUT HIS BACKGROUND? BETTER IF ELENA'S TOLD BEFORE SHE FINDS OUT.

I WON'T SAY HE'S SQUEAKY CLEAN. HE BECAME A PI WHEN HE TOOK ME.

BEFORE THAT... LET'S JUST SAY HE HAD EXPERIENCE ON THE OTHER SIDE OF THE LAW.

ENFORCEMENT WORK MAINLY. NOTHING THAT WOULD KEEP HIM FROM PACK MEMBERSHIP?

AND WHAT ABOUT YOU? IF YOUR DAD DECIDES TO STAY...

I STAY WITH HIM.

IS THAT WHAT YOU WANT?

TO BE WITH MY DAD? OF COURSE.

I MEAN YOUR DAD BEING PART OF THE PACK. IS THAT WHAT YOU WANT?

I THINK I COULD ADJUST.

GOOD.

THE END

Meanwhile at Stonehaven...

The Legacy

circa Bounty Hunt
2014

REESE ANDERSON
(AKA Reese Robinson, Reese Williams)

Born: April 3, 1987 as Reese Robinson.
Raised as Reese Williams.
Joined the Pack as Reese Anderson.

Hereditary werewolf, non-Pack,
origins: Australia
Joined: early 2009

Reese first came to the Pack's attention
when framed for man-killing by non-Pack
werewolves Liam Malloy and Ramon Santos. Reese
fled to Alaska, where he was mutilated by local
werewolves, losing part of two fingers on his
right hand.

Reese stayed with the Sorrentinos, under
Antonio's official and Nick's de facto guardianship.
He joined the Pack the following year, returned
to college and worked for Antonio's company.

At this time, Reese's reasons for fleeing
Australia are not a matter of Pack record.
They have been related to the current Alpha
(Elena Michaels) who will add them to this
record.

With Reese's consent, this record has been
updated with a brief account of his history.

Reese's mother was attacked and raped by
non-Pack Australian werewolves. She went public
with her story and while it was dismissed, it
caught the attention of the Australian Pack,
who sent Wes Robinson to kill her. Instead, the
two defied the Pack and hid under the surname
Williams.

Born: July 6, 1946.
Hereditary Pack werewolf.
Father: Dominic
Brothers: Gregory, Benedict
Son: Nicholas
Wards: Reese Anderson,
        Noah Stillwell

Antonio Sorrentino

On the death of his father, the Pack Alpha, Antonio formally renounced any intention to succeed Dominic and officially endorsed the ascension of Jeremy Danvers.

Early success in the technological market allowed Antonio to take control of the struggling family business and expand it into a multinational corporation. His success funded Jeremy's plan for nationwide monitoring of non-Pack werewolves. He also anonymously funded the scholarship that allowed Logan Jonsen to attend law school. The fact that he never actually looks at the Legacy allows his Alpha to officially note that without fear of discovery. It also allows his Alpha to include the photograph above, which might otherwise cause Antonio some embarrassment (and if you ever read this, Tonio, just remember the photo you submitted of me to my high school year book.)

While Antonio would claim that his focus was on his business rather than Pack duties, his Alpha will point out that Antonio not only acted as his advisor, but often seemed to coincidentally have business to conduct in areas of potential threats or near non-Pack werewolves requiring surveillance, which he managed to handle despite his busy work schedule. His contributions to the Pack were invaluable, even if he would staunchly claim otherwise.

NICOLAS SORRENTINO
(LKB)

Born: March 1, 1961

Hereditary Pack werewolf
Father: Antonio
Wards: Reese Anderson, Noah Stillwell

Nicholas Sorrentino

Nick played an instrumental role in the ascension of Jeremy Danvers. In the early years of that Alphahood, he assisted Clayton Danvers in disseminating and enforcing new policies regarding non–Pack werewolves. After Elena Michaels assumed the role of liaison with non–Pack werewolves, Nick extended his assistance in that area and, with Elena's ascent to Alphahood, he took on the role for himself.

While Nick's father, Antonio, accepted official guardianship of Reese Anderson and Noah Stillwell, Nick became their de facto guardian. He also mentored Morgan Walsh in the same capacity. For all three, he supervised their training and their assimilation into Pack life as well as supporting them in the development of their independent lives.

For years, the Pack struggled to expand its ranks, with minimal success. With Morgan, Reese and Noah, Pack membership finally reached a viable size. This success can be wholly attributed to Nick's efforts. He took three young werewolves, all from difficult backgrounds, none eager to join the Pack, and not only persuaded them to do so but turned them into full and loyal members, able to perform Pack duties and defend Pack territory despite their youth and inexperience.

Born: May 30, 1990 as Noah Stillwell.

Father: Joseph (Joey) Stillwell,

            former Pack member

Hereditary werewolf, non-Pack

Joined: early 2009

Noah came to the Pack on the death of his grandfather. Antonio Sorrentino accepted legal guardianship, while Nick Sorrentino has taken on the task of raising Noah through early adulthood. Noah has decided to drop the Stillwell name and now goes by Sorrentino.

In contrast to former Pack law and werewolf custom, Noah was raised by his human mother who was unaware of his werewolf bloodline. While the current Pack no longer opposes this practice, Noah's situation does illustrate some issues with it as outlined below.

Noah's grandfather (Dennis Stillwell) played an active role in his young life as, to a lesser extent, did his father, which alleviated the issue of human parenthood. Noah was told of his werewolf birthright as a young teen. His mother was an alcoholic who did not cease her alcohol consumption during pregnancy, leaving Noah with FAE (fetal alcohol effects) More on this below. His mother's alcoholism led to a difficult childhood for Noah, worsened when she married a man who very clearly did not want a stepson. While it could be argued that Noah suffered no more than any other child in such a circumstance, it is the Alpha's opinion that being a werewolf in a human family only exacerbated his sense of isolation. Therefore it could be argued that, in such a situation, removal of a werewolf child from his mother's care is still acceptable, even desirable, as it may no longer be in other circumstances.

FAE leaves Noah with various developmental issues. He is small and looks young for his age, and so it was decided that his new identification would set his birthdate a year younger, putting him back a year in school. He is easily frustrated and has difficulty concentrating, which makes school a struggle despite an above-average IQ. Further notes on how his condition affects his werewolf life can be found in a separate entry.

CHARLES GRAY

Born: August 9, 1960
Hereditary werewolf, non-Pack,
Australian origin

This record stands as a
potential application for Pack
membership. Upon approval, it will
be re-entered in the Legacy for
a member in good standing. If
not approved-or if the candidate
does not apply for membership-it
will be transferred to non-Pack
werewolf dossiers.

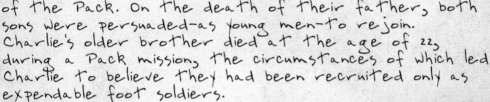

Charles (Charlie) was born into
the Australian Pack, younger son
of a long-standing member. On
the ascension of Gavin Wright,
his father took his two sons out
of the Pack. On the death of their father, both
sons were persuaded-as young men-to rejoin.
Charlie's older brother died at the age of 22,
during a Pack mission, the circumstances of which led
Charlie to believe they had been recruited only as
expendable foot soldiers.

Charlie left the Pack shortly after his brother's
death. However, his status-being born to the Pack
and later rejoining it-put him in the Pack's debt,
and he was obliged to perform enforcement duties
for the Pack in return for being permitted to
live in Australia. During this time, Charlie did not
limit his illegal activities to his Pack obligations, but
made his living as an enforcer engaged primarily in
criminal enterprises.

In 1988, Charlie fathered a daughter, Madison. She
lived with her mother and received financial support
from Charlie. While Madison had no early contact
with her father, she was given his name and
number to call in an emergency and did so upon the
murder of her mother in 1993. Charlie took custody
of his daughter at this time and gave up his
criminal endeavors, becoming a private investigator,
though he continued to work for the Australian
Pack as required.

In 2010, Charlie came to America with his daughter
on a matter involving Reese Anderson. That
incident is detailed elsewhere. It is expected he will
apply for Pack membership.

AUSTRALIAN PACK

WILLIAM TYNES, OF LONDON (ENGLAND). 1798

The first werewolves known to have settled in Australia did so in 1798, when the Tynes family of England —father William, sons John, James and Edward— emigrated voluntarily. The eldest Tynes son, John, had been incarcerated for murder, having been apprehended during a fatal brawl. English Pack law decreed that werewolves who were unable to evade capture or escape imprisonment must take their own lives before their first Change as captives (see entry on "Incarceration and Other Forms of Confinement.") John chose deportation to the Australian penal colony instead. The English Pack opposed his decision, arguing that the months-long voyage posed the same exposure risks at incarceration, but the Tynes family defied the Pack and left with John.

Upon arrival in Australia, the Tynes family founded their own Pack and bolstered its numbers by biting and turning other convicts. By the time other Packs made contact, the Australian one had become renowned in the territory for their viciousness and violence, extreme even by werewolf standards. They chose to operate their Pack as a criminal enterprise and have continued to do so to the modern day.

In the early nineteenth century, attempts were made by the English Pack to treat the Australians as colonists, imposing some rule of law on them while acknowledging their semi-independence. Visits resulted in an inexplicable number of casualties allegedly occurring on the voyage from England to the colony, the envoys —according to the Australian Pack— never reaching their destination. When attempts to enforce the Pack ban on marriage resulted in the loss of three Pack members, the English Pack decided to allow the Australians full independence from imperialistic oversight.

Structurally, the Australian Pack is comprised of several core families plus additional members, much like other Western Packs. It is led by an Alpha, which as in other Packs, is not typically a hereditary position. The Alpha may choose a successor and others may oppose that choice, though it appears that is done only in very rare instances and typically results in the mysterious disappearance of the opposing member. Unlike most modern Western Packs, the Australians allow the Alpha to mate. Daughters produced by that union remain in the Pack, where one will usually be betrothed to the next Alpha, and any remaining daughters will serve as household help for the Alpha's mate.

WELCOME TO THE OTHERWORLD

★ ★ ★

A Chronological Series List of Kelley Armstrong's Women of the Otherworld with Character Guide and a Guide to Half-Demon Abilities

Legend: **novel**, *short story*, novella

TABLE OF CONTENTS

★ ★ ★

Chronological Series List

The Otherworld

Rebirth - Aaron, "Tales of the Otherworld"
Infusion - Malcolm, "Men of the Otherworld"
Savage - Clay, "Men of the Otherworld"
Ascension - Clay, "Men of the Otherworld"
Bewitched - Eve, "Tales of the Otherworld"
Demonology - Talia, "Otherworld Nights"
Birthright - Logan, "Tales of the Otherworld"
Beginnings - Clay & Elena, "Tales of the Otherworld"
Becoming* - Elena
Case of the Half-Demon Spy - Adam, "Otherworld Chills"
Expectations - Lucas, "Tales of the Otherworld"
Truth and Consequences - Elena
Territorial - Karl
Bitten - Elena
Ghosts - Jeremy, "Tales of the Otherworld"
Escape - Eve
Stolen - Elena
Dime Store Magic - Paige
Industrial Magic - Paige
Wedding Bell Hell - Paige, "Tales of the Otherworld"
Haunted - Eve
Adventurer - Kenneth
Chaotic - Hope, "Otherworld Chills"
Bargain - Xavier
Broken - Elena
Case of El Chupacabra - Lucas, "Tales of the Otherworld"

No Humans Involved - Jaime
Framed - Nick
Twilight - Cassandra, "Otherworld Nights"
Stalked - Clay, "Otherworld Nights"
Personal Demon - Hope & Lucas
Chivalrous - Reese, "Otherworld Nights"
The Ungrateful Dead - Jaime, "Otherworld Secrets"
Living with the Dead - Multiple Narrators
Kitsunegari - Jeremy, "Men of the Otherworld"
Zen and the Art of Vampirism - Zoe, "Otherworld Secrets"
Angelic - Eve, "Otherworld Secrets"
Learning Curve - Zoe, "Evolve"
Lucifer's Daughter - Hope, "Otherworld Nights"
Checkmate - Elena
Recruit - Elena
Frostbitten - Elena
The List - Zoe, "Evolve 2"
Hidden - Elena, "Otherworld Nights"
Forbidden - Elena, "Otherworld Secrets"
Counterfeit Magic - Paige, "Otherworld Secrets"
Off-Duty Angel - Eve, "Otherworld Chills"
V Plates - Nick, "Blood Lite 3"
Amityville Horrible - Jaime, "Otherworld Chills"
Sorry … the Hardest Word - Zoe, "Otherworld Chills"
Waking the Witch - Savannah & Adam
Spell Bound - Savannah
Thirteen - Savannah and others
From Russia with Love - Elena, "Otherworld Nights"
Vanishing Act - Savannah, "Otherworld Nights"
Brazen - Nick, "Otherworld Chills"

Bounty Hunt* - Reese
Forsaken - Elena
Life After Theft - Hope, "Otherworld Secrets"
The Puppy Plan - Logan Danvers, "Otherworld Chills"
Driven - Elena
Baby Boom - Paige, "Otherworld Chills"
*Graphic novella

DARKEST POWERS/DARKNESS RISING
(young adult, set in Otherworld universe)
Dangerous - Derek, "Darkest Powers Tales"
Kat - Katiana
The Summoning - Chloe
Divided - Derek, "Darkest Powers Tales"
The Awakening - Chloe
Disenchanted - Tori, "Darkest Powers Tales"
The Reckoning - Chloe
Facing Facts - Chloe, "Darkest Powers Tales"
Hunting Kat - Katiana, "Kisses from Hell"
Belonging - Derek, "Darkest Powers Tales"
The Gathering - Maya
The Calling - Maya
The Rising - Maya
Atoning – Chloe

CHARACTER GUIDE
Characters given alphabetically, by last name.
Major/significant series characters only.

Adams, Hope.
Expisco (Chaos) half-demon.
Chaotic, **No Humans Involved, Personal Demon, Living with the Dead, Spell Bound, Thirteen,** *Lucifer's Daughter,* Forsaken, Life After Theft

Callas, Vanessa.
Aduro (Fire) Half-demon.
Brazen, Forsaken, Driven

Cortez, Benicio.
Sorcerer.
Industrial Magic, *Wedding Bell Hell, The Case of El Chupacabra,* **Personal Demon, Spell Bound**

Cortez, Lucas Diego.
Sorcerer.
Expectations, **Dime Store Magic, Industrial Magic,** *Wedding Bell Hell,* **Haunted,** *The Case of El Chupacabra,* **Personal Demon,** Counterfeit Magic, **Spell Bound, Thirteen**

Danvers, Clayton.
Werewolf.
Savage, Ascension, *Birthright,* Beginnings, **Bitten, Stolen, Industrial Magic, Broken,** *Stalked, Checkmate, Recruit,*

Frostbitten, Hidden, Forbidden, **Spell Bound, Thirteen**, Brazen, Bounty Hunt, Forsaken, The Puppy Plan, Driven

Danvers, Jeremy Malcolm Edwards.
Werewolf, Kitsunegari.
Savage, Ascension, *Birthright,* Beginnings, *Ghosts,* **Bitten, Stolen, Industrial Magic, Broken, No Humans Involved,** *Kitsunegari*, Hidden, Forbidden, Amityville Horrible, **Spell Bound, Thirteen,** Bounty Hunt, Forsaken, Driven

Danvers, Kate.
Werewolf.
Hidden, Bounty Hunt, Forsaken, The Puppy Plan, Driven

Danvers, Logan.
Werewolf.
Hidden, Bounty Hunt, Forsaken, The Puppy Plan, Driven

Danvers, Malcolm.
Werewolf.
Infusion, Savage, Ascension, *Territorial,* **Thirteen,** Brazen, Bounty Hunt, Forsaken, Driven

Darnell, Aaron.
Vampire.
Rebirth, **Stolen, Industrial Magic,** *Twilight*

DuCharme, Cassandra.
Vampire.
Rebirth, **Stolen, Industrial Magic,** *The Case of El Chupacabra, Twilight,* **Spell Bound**

Findlay, John (Finn).

Necromancer.
Living with the Dead

Haig, Jasper (Jaz).
Unknown, "human chameleon".
Personal Demon, Spell Bound

James, Madison.
Human.
Bounty Hunt, Driven

Jonsen, Logan.
Werewolf.
Birthright, Beginnings**, Bitten**

Levine, Eve.
Witch/Aspicio half-demon/Angel.
Bewitched, *Expectations, Escape,* **Industrial Magic, Haunted, No Human Involved,** Angelic, **Thirteen,** *Off-Duty Angel*

Levine, Savannah Constance.
Witch/sorcerer.
Escape, **Stolen, Dime Store Magic, Industrial Magic, Haunted,** *Wedding Bell Hell, The Case of El Chupacabra,* **No Humans Involved,** *The Ungrateful Dead,* Counterfeit Magic, **Waking the Witch, Spell Bound, Thirteen,** Vanishing Act

Marsten, Karl.
Werewolf.
Territorial, **Bitten,** Chaotic, **No Humans Involved, Personal Demon, Living with the Dead,** *Lucifer's Daughter,* **Spell**

O'Donnell, Leah.
>Volo (telekinetic) half-demon.
>**Stolen, Dime Store Magic, Waking the Witch**

Okalik, Kenneth.
>Shaman. Ayami (spirit guide): Taira.
>**Stolen,** *Adventurer*

Peltier, Robyn.
>Human.
>**Living with the Dead**

Reese, Xavier.
>Evanidus (teleportation) half-demon.
>*Bargain,* **Stolen, Broken**

Smith, Rhys.
>Clairvoyant.
>**Living With the Dead**

Sorenson, Griffin.
>Ferratus (iron) half-demon.
>**Industrial Magic, Personal Demon, Spell Bound**

Sorrentino, Antonio.
>Werewolf.
>Savage, Ascension, Beginnings, **Bitten, Broken,** Bounty Hunt, Forsaken, Driven

Sorrentino, Dominic.
>Werewolf.
>*Infusion,* Savage, Ascension

Vegas, Jaime.
   Necromancer.
   Industrial Magic, Haunted, Broken, No Humans Involved, *The Ungrateful Dead, Kitsunegari,* Amityville Horrible, **Spell Bound, Thirteen**, Driven

Walsh, Morgan.
   Werewolf.
   Frostbitten, Forbidden, Forsaken

Williams, Reese. (Born Reese Robinson, later Reese Anderson)
   Werewolf.
   Chivalrous, **Frostbitten,** Hidden, Brazen, Bounty Hunt, Forsaken, Driven

Winterbourne, Paige Katherine.
   Witch.
   The Case of the Half-Demon Spy, **Stolen, Dime Store Magic, Industrial Magic,** *Wedding Bell Hell, The Case of El Chupacabra,* **Personal Demon**, Counterfeit Magic, **Waking the Witch, Spell Bound, Thirteen,** Baby Boom

Winterbourne, Ruth.
   Witch.
   Stolen

GUIDE TO HALF-DEMON ABILITIES

In the Otherworld, the true form of demons is unknown, but they exist in the physical and spiritual world and fit into two categories: eudemons and cacodemons. Eudemons are non-chaotic, while cacodemons enjoy trying to screw up the human world and are likely the kind of demon one would run into.

Half-Demons are the children of human women and demons, who take human form to sire children. Depending on their demon father, half-demons can have a variety of powers and strengths. Powers manifest commonly between the ages of twelve and twenty.

Strength of half-demons is measured on a hierarchy, with one being considered a particular rank when he or she has manifested a power at that rank. This rank is somewhat inborn, although one's full potential can be reached through a combination of physical maturity and practice.

TYPES OF HALF-DEMONS
Elemental, Dimensional & Physical

ELEMENTAL

Fire - can produce fire through physical contact

Ranks:
Igneus - can cause first degree burns, may be able to produce sparks
Aduro - can cause second degree burns, can ignite flammable material
Exustio - can cause third degree burns, can incinerate objects

Otherworld Characters: Adam Vasic (Exustio)
Tempestras - can control weather, calling wind, rain or lightning

Otherworld Characters: Robert Vasic, Troy Morgan

DIMENSIONAL

Telekinetic - can move objects without physical means

Ranks:
Migro - range: within sight
      object size: small (~10lbs max)
      displacement: minimal (less than 6 in)
Agito - range: within sight
      object size: not larger/heaver than self
      displacement: ~10 feet max
Volo - range: ~50 yards (if not in sight, must be able to picture object and
      its placement)
      object size: unknown
      displacement: ~20 feet max

Otherworld Characters: Leah O'Donnell (Volo), Jesse Aanes (Agito)

Teleportation - can move self instantaneously

Ranks:
Tripudio - target range: within sight
      direction: horizontal only
      distance: ~12in max.
Evanidus - target range: within sight
      direction: horizontal only
      distance: ~10 feet max.
Abeo - target range: anywhere within ~50 feet
      direction: horizontal and vertical
      distance: ~50 feet max.

Otherworld Characters: Xavier Reese (Evanidus)

PHYSICAL

Vision - enhanced visual abilities and control

Ranks:
note: each rank also has the abilities of the previous
Acies - enhanced visual range
Conspicio - can induce temporary blindness
Aspicio - can see through solid objects

Otherworld Characters: Eve Levine (Aspicio)

Ferratus (iron) - can make his or her skin as hard as iron

Otherworld Characters: Griffin Sorenson

HTTP://WWW.KELLEYARMSTRONG.COM

Photo credit: Kathryn Hollinrake.

Kelley Armstrong has been telling stories since before she could write. Her earliest written efforts were disastrous. If asked for a story about girls and dolls, hers would invariably feature undead girls and evil dolls, much to her teachers' dismay. Today, she continues to spin tales of ghosts and demons and werewolves, while safely locked away in her basement writing dungeon. She lives in southwestern Ontario with her husband, kids and far too many pets.

Xaviere Daumarie is a French artist who learned English and Japanese so she could read more books. Following a degree in Japanese Language and Civilization from the Inalco in Paris, she began freelance publishing work. She now divides her artistic time between two styles, a realistic one for all things Otherworld and a cartoony style for her own books created under the pseudonym Angilram.

She travels back and forth between France and Canada with her Cintiq and a suitcase full of tea.

She can easily be bribed with chocolate, tea and books.

HTTP://WWW.XAVIEREDAUMARIE.COM
http://www.angilram.com

BECOMING

OTHERWORLD
KELLEY ARMSTRONG
ILLUSTRATED BY XAVIERE DAUMARIE

Elena Michaels has just been bitten by her boyfriend, psycho werewolf Clay Danvers. As the werewolf curse is slowly taking over her body and mind, she clings to the last shreds of her humanity, scared that her life will never be the same again.

As per readers' request, finally the tale of Elena's Bite, as a graphic novel.
Becoming covers the darkest part of Elena's introduction to life as a werewolf, and fills in an important chapter in the *Otherworld* story.

The Otherworld, a series of novels written by Kelley Armstrong,

60098703R00059

Made in the USA
Charleston, SC
22 August 2016